Staying with
Grandmother

Staying with
Grandmother

Barbara Baker

PICTURES BY

Judith Byron Schachner

Dutton Children's Books
NEW YORK

Text copyright © 1994 by Barbara A. Baker
Illustrations copyright © 1994 by Judith Byron Schachner

Library of Congress Cataloging-in-Publication Data

Baker, Barbara, date.
Staying with grandmother / by Barbara Baker;
illustrated by Judith Byron Schachner.—1st ed.
p. cm.
Summary: Clair feels less homesick after Grandmother
reads a favorite story and introduces a new friend.
ISBN 0-525-44603-6
[1. Grandmothers—Fiction.   2. Homesickness—Fiction.]
I. Schachner, Judith Byron, ill.   II. Title.
PZ7.B16922St   1994   [E]—dc20   93-13749   CIP   AC

Published in the United States 1994 by Dutton Children's Books,
a division of Penguin Books USA Inc.
375 Hudson Street, New York, New York 10014

Printed in Hong Kong
First Edition
1 3 5 7 9 10 8 6 4 2

*For Marilyn and Clair
and Jennifer*
B.A.B.

For Helen, our Grandmother
J.B.S.

Contents

SAYING GOOD-BYE

I am not going to cry.

My mother and my father

are getting ready to say good-bye.

My mother says,

"Be a good girl, Clair."

She hugs me.

My father says,

"Take good care of Grandmother, Clair.

We will be back soon."

I do not want them to go at all.

But I try to smile.

My mother and father kiss me

one last time.

And then they leave.

When they are gone,

I feel so sad.

But I can see that Grandmother

looks sad, too.

She gives me a hug.

I hug her back.

MY ROOM

Grandmother's house is old.

My mother lived here

when she was a little girl.

I will sleep upstairs in the room

that was my mother's.

Grandmother is making dinner.

She asks me if I would like

to put away my things.

I say, "Yes."

Upstairs I open the wrong door.

I find steps going to the <u>attic.</u>

It is dark up there.

I close the door quickly.

Then I find my room.

I see a bed and a funny old dresser
with big deep drawers.

A rocking chair is in the corner.

Across the room, there is a window.

I crawl over the bed

and push the curtains open.

I can see right into a big leafy tree.

A little bird flies from branch to branch.

He looks at me.

"This room is my tree house,"

I tell him.

"My real home is far away."

The little bird flies off.

I turn away from the window.

I open my suitcase

and start to unpack.

"Clair," Grandmother calls.

"Time for dinner."

"I'm coming," I say.

On my way downstairs,

I run past the attic door.

DINNER

Dinner smells good.

I wash my hands,

and then I help Grandmother.

She says I can set the table.

I do that at home.

Grandmother's dishes

have tiny flowers on them.

They are prettier than ours.

I remember to fold the napkins.

"The table looks very nice, Clair,"

says Grandmother.

"Thank you," I say.

I am glad that I did a good job.

Now we are ready to eat.

We have macaroni and cheese.

It is good.

But I like the way my mother

makes it better.

She puts in more cheese.

I wonder what my mother and father

are having for dinner.

I wish I was with them.

Grandmother says,

"Would you like to go

for a walk with me later?"

"Yes," I say.

"Good," says Grandmother.

"I would like you to meet

a special friend of mine."

When we finish our dinner,

I help Grandmother wash the dishes.

Then Grandmother says,

"Are you ready for our walk?"

"Yes," I say. "Who is

your special friend?"

"You'll see," says Grandmother.

EVENING WALK

It is not dark yet,

but the sun is going down.

We walk along slowly.

The cool evening air feels good.

I can smell flowers and grass and earth.

Sometimes I smell other people's dinners.

We walk until we come

to a big house on the corner.

There is a girl sitting on the porch.

My grandmother says,

"Hello, Jennifer. This is Clair."

Jennifer jumps down from the porch.

"Hello," she says to my grandmother.

Then she looks at me.

"Hi, Clair," she says.

"I have a skateboard and a bike

and skates and *four* brothers.

But no girls live around here."

Jennifer smiles.

"Do you want to play with me

tomorrow?"

I look at Jennifer.

She has Band-Aids on both

of her knees and on one elbow.

There is a scratch on her chin.

I smile back at her. "Yes," I say.

I hope Grandmother has Band-Aids.

Grandmother says,

"Come over after breakfast, Jennifer."

Then we all say good-bye.

It's getting dark.

On the way home,

I remember something.

"Grandmother," I say,

"we didn't meet your special friend."

"My special friend is Jennifer,"

says Grandmother.

"Jennifer?" I say.

"Yes," says Grandmother.

Then she laughs because

I am surprised.

"But I hope she will be

your special friend, Clair."

"I hope so, too," I say.

BEDTIME

Now it is dark.

I turn on the lamp in my room.

It makes a cozy glow.

But I feel sad anyway.

I miss my mother and father.

I miss my old bear.

He is at home.

I forgot to pack him.

I see a book on the night table.

The cover is faded blue.

It is called *Alice in Wonderland.*

I know that story.

When I open the book,

I see the name *Marilyn*

on the first page.

Marilyn is my mother.

I touch the name gently.

I want to cry.

Grandmother comes in.

"Would you like me to read

to you, Clair?" she says.

I nod my head.

Grandmother sits in the rocking chair.

She opens *Alice in Wonderland*

and begins to read.

I snuggle down under the quilt.

Grandmother finishes the first chapter.

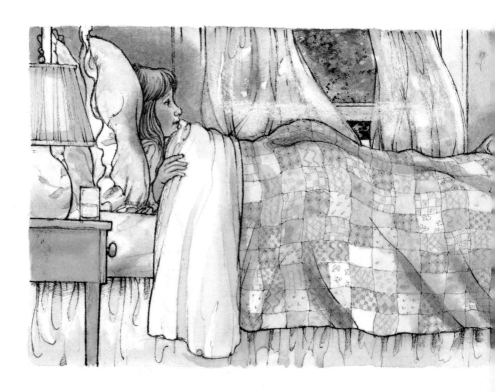

She says,

"Your mother loved this book

when she was your age.

I know something else that she loved.

I will go and get it for you."

I wait in bed.

I hear Grandmother open a door.

I hear footsteps going up to the attic.

I wait and wait.

Finally Grandmother comes back.

"I found White Rabbit

in your mother's old toy box,"

she says.

"Oh," I say. "He is wonderful.

Was he really my mother's?"

"Yes," says Grandmother.

"And she thought

he was wonderful, too."

Grandmother hands

White Rabbit to me.

"I am glad you like him," she says.

"Good night, Clair." She kisses me.

Then she goes downstairs.

I am alone in my room.

I hug White Rabbit.

He is old, but his fur is still soft.

"Oh, White Rabbit," I say.

"Did my mother pretend to be Alice

when you were her rabbit?"

White Rabbit's whiskers tickle my nose.

I think about my mother and father.

I think about Jennifer.

I hope she will let me try

her skateboard.

I hope she will be my friend.

I think about *Alice in Wonderland*

and the toy box in the attic

and the little bird in my tree.

I hug White Rabbit tight.

I think tomorrow will be

a good day.